THE SADDLE BAG HERO

Siân Lewis

Illustrated by Karen Heywood

Young Piper Books

First published 1984 by Hamish Hamilton Children's Books
This Young Piper Edition first published 1990 by
Pan Books Ltd, Cavaye Place, London SW10 9PG
9 8 7 6 5
© 1984 by Siân Lewis
Illustrations © 1984 by Karen Heywood
ISBN 0 330 31288 X

Printed and bound in Great Britain by
Richard Clay Ltd, Bungay, Suffolk

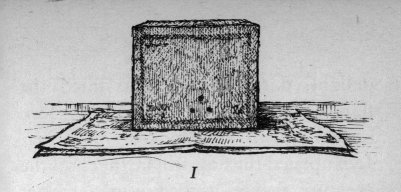

I

The Birthday Present

LYN WANTED AN Alsatian for her tenth birthday. She wanted an Alsatian as big as herself with a terrifying growl. She wanted an Alsatian who'd scare the living daylights out of String who sat behind her in class.

On her birthday morning Lyn woke up early. She sat up in bed and listened hard till she heard scratching noises from the living-room below. She ran downstairs.

On a sheet of newspaper on the living-room table stood a medium-sized cardboard box. Lyn gave a squeal of delight, darted across and lifted the flap. The scratching stopped. Two scared brown eyes looked up at her. Lyn opened the flap still farther and the creature inside backed into a corner shaking from top to toe.

Lyn took hold of it and lifted it out. It had cream and brown fur just like an Alsatian, only the colours ran in uneven bands around its body so it looked like a giant bumble-bee. It had four short kicking legs, but no sign of a tail. It lifted its nose to sniff at Lyn and she saw two rows of tiny rat-like teeth.

"A guinea-pig!" Lyn cried and collapsed on to the settee in disgust.

That frightened the guinea-pig. It didn't growl, though. It didn't bark till the house echoed. It just gave one small nervous squeak.

"I'm not going to hurt you, silly!"

Lyn took pity and put out her hand to stroke him. The guinea-pig was running in circles round her lap. He tried diving underneath her arm and burying himself behind the cushion. She tucked him under her chin and felt his heart thumping away against her chest.

That's where he was when Mum came in blinking and screwing up her eyes. Mum was short-sighted. It wasn't until she was sitting next to Lyn on the settee that she spotted the new pet.

"Like him?" Her face brightened.

"He's all right." Lyn didn't bother to lift her head.

"You weren't still thinking of an Alsatian, were you?" Mum asked anxiously. "Dad and I told you . . ."

"I know," said Lyn.

"The house is too small and I'm out working all day."

"I know."

"It wouldn't be fair."

Dad was whistling 'Happy Birthday' on the stairs. He kissed Lyn on the top of her head, then reached for a piece of carrot from the box and held it out. The guinea-pig drew back sharply and slid

down under Lyn's hand.

"Now don't you be like that with me," Dad said. "I've had guinea-pigs before, you know."

"I'll give it to him," Lyn sighed. She lowered the guinea-pig till he was sitting comfortably in the crook of her arm. She left him there till he had settled and wasn't wriggling round clawing at her nightie. Then she held out the carrot. The nose twitched. It went on twitching for quite a long time before its owner finally plucked up courage to snatch the carrot from Lyn's hand, drop it on her nightie and then eat it up.

"Good!" Dad crouched down in front of the guinea-pig. "We'll have to think of a name for him now. What shall we call him?"

"Alsatian," said Lyn.

Mum and Dad exchanged glances.
Dad pushed his way in between Mum
and Lyn on the settee and took the
guinea-pig on to his lap.

"What about Columbus?" He
nudged Lyn. "I used to have a guinea-

pig called Columbus. We called him that because he fell into the sink one day when my Mum was doing the washing-up and sailed across on a plastic butter-dish."

"This one hasn't fallen into the sink," said Lyn.

"Mmmmm." Dad put his head to one side and studied the guinea-pig who was sitting watching them all with small frightened eyes. "Shakin' Stevens?" he suggested.

"Shakin' Stevens!" Lyn exploded and the guinea-pig made a leap for shelter in Dad's sleeve.

"Hey!" said Dad.

Lyn gave a whoop of laughter. The guinea-pig was stuck and his back legs were wriggling and kicking.

"Get him out!" puffed Dad.

"Come on, Alsatian," Lyn spluttered. "Come to Lyn." She tried to catch hold of him, but it only made him more frightened and he wriggled farther in.

Mum was laughing so much the whole settee was vibrating.

"You two women, stop laughing!" Dad had gone red in the face. "Do something! Guinea-pigs can die if they're frightened."

Everyone went quiet. Dad carefully unbuttoned his pyjama jacket and slipped out his free arm. The guinea-pig squeaked.

"Don't bend your arm!" whispered

Lyn. "It makes the sleeve tighter. You're hurting him."

She stroked Alsatian gently, both the part of him that was under the sleeve and the back part that was clawing at Dad's arm.

"Straighten your elbow."

She slipped the jacket down over Dad's shoulder till Alsatian's nose came into view. The sleeve was gathered tight round his middle with his nose poking out at one end and his back legs at the other. Mum took one look and collapsed in a giggling heap.

"Don't! You're frightening him." Lyn felt all hot and bothered and poor Alsatian was still wedged tight. "I'll have to give a sharp pull." She brought her face up close to Alsatian and whispered "Don't worry", in his ear.

Alsatian was so frightened to see this

huge face bearing down on him that he
shot back and suddenly most of him slid
out at the other end of the sleeve. Lyn
caught him and there he was, ruffled
and trembling, but snug in the crook of
her arm.

Dad whistled with relief and tossed
his pyjama jacket on the floor.

"Clean pyjamas tonight," he said. "I'm not wearing them after that creature."

"Don't be rude," said Lyn.

Mum sat up wiping her eyes.

"Let's call him Bandit," she said in a quavery voice.

"Daft name," said Dad.

"Well he was a sort of one-armed bandit, when . . ." And Mum was off again.

Lyn laughed too.

"Don't tell me you like your mother's choice of name," said Dad, sounding pleased all the same.

Lyn shook her head.

"He's going to be Alsatian," she said firmly.

Mum grew serious in a moment. It was Lyn's birthday, so she wasn't going to lose her temper. Instead she looked up at the ceiling and clamped her hands tight between her knees.

"How would you like it," she said without looking at Lyn, "if we called you Simon?"

Lyn snorted so loudly that poor Alsatian would have dived off her lap again if she hadn't been holding him tight.

"Don't you dare call me Simon," she said.

Simon, or String as he was known because of his immensely long legs, was Lyn's arch-enemy in school.

"Calling a guinea-pig Alsatian," Mum said, "is just as insulting as calling you by a boy's name."

"No!" Lyn looked down at her pet who, by this time, was trying to sleep on her arm. "He's the same colour as an Alsatian. Anyway I like the name. And I like him too."

"Alsatian it is then." Dad squeezed her shoulder.

"I still think Alsatian's a silly name for a guinea-pig, just as Simon's a silly name for a girl." Mum peeped round at Lyn from the corner of her eye.

Lyn grinned. Little did Mum know, but the guinea-pig had to be called Alsatian for a very good reason.

That reason was Simon-String.

2

String's Bike

IT HAD ALL started on String's birthday.

String had had a bike. Now that he was almost as tall as Mr Hughes, their teacher, he hadn't just had a Grifter or a Burner. No, String had had a super full-size red and white six-speed bike with a special aluminium frame. It was very slightly second-hand, but String had cleaned and polished it so well that you'd never have guessed.

Lyn hadn't seen him arrive at school

on the bike. The first thing she knew about it was when String's long legs reached out under his own desk, under her chair, and kicked her feet.

"Don't!" Lyn grumbled over her shoulder.

"I've got a new bike," he said.

"So what?"

At break-time he fetched it from the shed at the side of the school and the whole class gathered round him except for Lyn and her friend Vicky.

"He's a show-off," Vicky said.

String came over and parked the bike right in front of them.

"What d'you think of that then?"

"Rubbish," said Lyn.

"O.K." String, in a huff, stood over them hands on hips. "What are you going to have on your birthday that's so special?"

"I'm going to have. . ." Lyn racked her brains. "I'm going to have an Alsatian."

"You're not!" String's jaw dropped.

"Are you going to have an Alsatian?" Suddenly the famous bike was forgotten in a clamour of excited voices. A policeman had come to school the week before with Bold, his Alsatian, who had impressed everyone by sniffing out a key, a sock and an old rubber ball hidden by his owner in the yard.

"I'd love to have an Alsatian," sighed Sharon Rees.

"She's not going to have an Alsatian," scoffed String. "She's only got a small house and anyway her Mum's out working all day."

String wasn't daft. That was exactly what Mum and Dad said when Lyn got home. But she had gone on hoping and hoping that, when she came downstairs on her birthday morning, she'd find a huge big dog lying across the mat who'd jump up barking to greet her. Instead she had a guinea-pig, a quiet little guinea-pig who at this very moment was sleeping in a warm bundle against her arm.

Lyn got gingerly to her feet. She carried Alsatian upstairs and made him a bed in her slipper while she got dressed. He blinked sleepily and pushed his nose into the pink fur.

"Bring him down when you're ready," Dad called. "I've got a hutch for him."

The hutch was a white box that Dad had made and painted secretly in the shed. He'd also made a wooden frame covered in wire which fitted over the door of the hutch so that Alsatian could go for a run in the fresh air. When Lyn came downstairs, the hutch and frame were already in place on the patch of lawn in the back yard.

"Oh, that's good!" she cried.

She opened the top of the hutch. In one half there was a pile of clean straw bedding. She set Alsatian down on top of it. He sniffed in an interested fashion, then slipped out of the door into the run and started nibbling the grass.

Dad gave Lyn a water bottle with a tube attached to it. She filled it from the

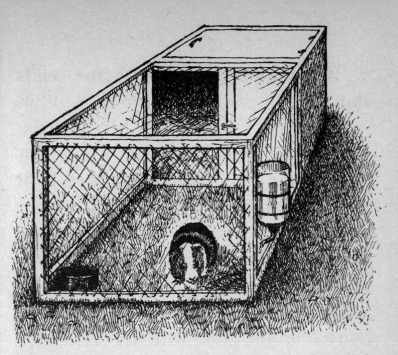

tap, wedged it upside down in the wire and wiggled the tube under Alsatian's nose.

"Water!" she called, but Alsatian just shuffled away and carried on eating.

Dad had bought a small earthenware dish as well. Lyn filled it with dried guinea-pig food and set it in the corner of the run. They both crouched down to watch Alsatian.

"He's not bothering with the seeds and things," said Lyn.

"He will," said Dad. "He'll have nibbled the grass bare by the time you come home from school and then he'll need something to fill his tum."

"Alsatian!" called Lyn and she pushed her fingers through the wire to stroke him.

Mum brought out her breakfast and Lyn sat on the grass with her cornflakes on her knee. Alsatian poked his nose through the mesh.

"Here!" Lyn gave him a soggy cornflake, but he let it drop and went back to his grass. He only stopped eating once and that was when the front doorbell disturbed him.

"That'll be Vicky," Lyn explained to him. "She's my friend."

She looked over her shoulder and saw

26

Vicky come tearing through the back door, her face round and shiny and her brown curls wobbling all over her head.

"Where is he?"

Lyn pointed at the stripy creature pulling at a juicy blade of grass in the corner of the run. Vicky stared.

"It's a guinea-pig!" Her face fell.

"Yes . . ."

"I asked your Mum if you'd had an Alsatian and she laughed and said, 'Yes. Sort of.'"

"He's the same colour as an Alsatian," said Lyn.

"But he's a guinea-pig!"

"I know," Lyn said testily. "I know he's a guinea-pig, but his name is Alsatian." She lifted the edge of the run, brought the guinea-pig out and deposited him on Vicky's lap.

Vicky put out her hand and Alsatian sniffed at it.

"It's O.K.," said Lyn. "He won't bite. He's just sniffing for grass, that's all."

Alsatian turned round. Vicky tried stroking him, but he'd seen the delicious green stuff just by her knee and headed straight for it. He slid down on to the grass, waddled round the far side of the run and settled down to eat.

Vicky giggled. "He's funny."

"He's not. He's lovely." Lyn crept towards him, picked him up and kissed him on the tip of the nose. Mum was at the back door calling them for school, so she put Alsatian back in his run and said goodbye. Alsatian poked his nose through the wire. "See! He knows me already."

"Lyn!" called Mum. She had her bag and coat over her arm.

"'Bye, Alsatian," said Lyn.

"Be good," said Vicky.

Lyn ran straight through the house grabbing her school bag as she ran. Mum combed her hair for her as she dashed past and put the band in place, but Lyn didn't have time to wash or clean her teeth. She and Vicky were late and galloping down the road.

They had forgotten about String. All the talk was of guinea-pigs. Jenny had brought a guinea-pig to school once. It had shot into hiding as soon as it set eyes on anyone. Mr Hughes had said it needed more handling to give it confidence.

"Alsatian's more confident already," said Lyn. "This morning when I opened the box, he was terrified, but he's got to know me ever so quickly. He . . . Ouch!" Vicky had nudged her. At the same time Lyn saw the danger. It was String, propped against the school gate. "O-o-oh!" She let out a long breath.

"What shall we do?" muttered Vicky. Both girls slowed.

"Avoid him . . ."

It was too late. String was heading towards them. He skidded to a halt and pushed his bike across the pavement, blocking their way.

"You didn't get an Alsatian, did you?" he demanded.

Lyn looked at Vicky and lifted her chin.

"I did," she said.

"She didn't," he said to Vicky.

"Yes, she did." Vicky pulled herself up and Lyn just had time to grab her friend's hand and drag her off before she gave the game away. Vicky had a habit of looking too mysterious.

They darted round String's bike and back on to the pavement just as the school bell rang. Lyn looked back over her shoulder as they ran towards the gate. String was still there sitting astride the bike and staring after her. Suddenly he pushed off and came whizzing by.

"You didn't," he shouted as he went past. "You didn't get an Alsatian. Bet you didn't. I'll ask your Mum."

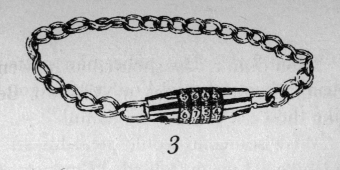

3

String Lies in Wait

LYN AND VICKY stuck together like limpets all day. It was the best way to avoid awkward questions. When P.C. Jones came for bike drill, they were sitting on the kerb at the side of the yard. In the excitement of Lyn's birthday they had left their bikes at home.

"Don't forget your bikes next week, Lyn and Vicky," P.C. Jones called. "I'm going to stamp them so you can recognise them if they're stolen."

"I've got a chain lock." String produced it from his pocket. He was showing off as usual.

"Good lad." The policeman patted String's back wheel. "You've got a good bike there. It pays to be careful."

"Wish someone would steal his stupid bike," Lyn mumbled. "I'm sick of hearing about it."

String swooped past, almost brushing Lyn's toes.

"Silly boy!" squawked Vicky in Mrs Davies, the infant teacher's, voice. "Silly boy! Put that bike away."

But it was the end of the afternoon and String didn't put his bike away. Once P.C. Jones had gone, it wasn't worth going back into class so String rode no-hands round the school yard.

"Oh, go home!" Lyn snapped at him as he sped past for the tenth time.

"You go home," he bawled back.

"We're going to Lyn's party at the Wimpy," yelled Vicky.

"So?" He circled the netball posts.

"We've got to wait for Lyn's Mum to come, haven't we?"

"So've I."

Vicky took a breath to shout back, then somehow it got bottled up inside her and she turned as red as a beetroot. String laughed.

"Why d'you want to see my Mum?" Lyn demanded.

String tapped his nose in an irritating way. Lyn and Vicky made a rush for him, but he pedalled off at top speed to the far end of the yard.

"I'm going to ask your Mum about the Alsatian," he shouted from a safe distance. "I'm going to ask your Mum."

Vicky's eyes were nearly popping out in alarm.

"O.K." Lyn shouted quickly. "You ask her. I don't mind."

The bell rang and the rest of the school flowed out trapping Sting in his corner. Lyn looked round for Sharon, Jenny and Rose, the other three girls who were coming to the party. She beckoned them over to the gate.

"We'll have to get into the car double quick," Lyn whispered to Vicky. She stood on the pavement and searched the stream of cars for Mum's red Mini. Mum didn't finish work till half past three, so she was never on time.

The crowd in the yard thinned. String rode over and stopped with one hand on the gate. He watched.

"What's the matter with you?" Vicky said crossly. "Want to come to the party?"

"I'll lend you a party dress." Sharon, who had changed into pink Bermudas

and a pink top in the cloakroom, waved
her school bag at him.

"Come on, String!" yelled the rest of
the girls.

String grinned and pressed his face against the railings.

"Why are you having a party in the Wimpy then?" he asked Lyn. "Why aren't you having it at home?"

"Because," said Lyn, hand on hip, "Mum's working and she hasn't got time to prepare it, that's why."

"Why didn't you have it at home so we could see your Alsatian?"

"*We?*" said Sharon.

"*You're* not coming," said Vicky.

"Lyn'll bring the Alsatian to the park to show us," put in Jenny.

Lyn flushed. A secret's not a secret if you tell everyone, but she felt mean about the other girls. Still, she knew they'd understand when she explained about String. String was far too clever and too big for his boots. It wouldn't do him any harm to think he was wrong for once. 38

Something jingled against the gate. She looked round. String was fixing the chain lock to his bike. He was going to join them on the pavement and interrogate Mum! Lyn glanced at Vicky in desperation. Vicky opened her mouth, then closed it and started nibbling worriedly at her thumb-nail.

"Where are you going?" Sharon asked String.

"Nowhere." String came out through the gate and propped himself against the post. His long legs spread out across the pavement and nearly tripped up Stevie Baker who was on his way home from the Junior High.

"Hey!" growled Stevie.

"Sorry!" String straightened.

"Watch it!" Stevie Baker squared his shoulders. He was small, wiry and about half String's size though he was nearly twelve.

"I didn't mean to," said String.

"I should think so too." Stevie spotted String's bike. "That yours?"

"Yes."

Sharon groaned and rolled her eyes. The girls all expected String to go droning on and on about his precious bike. But String didn't.

"Give us a ride," said Stevie.

"I've got to go home." String backed sharply through the gate with Stevie following.

"Give us a ride then," said Stevie. "Just a quick one."

"I've got to go home," said String crouching down and undoing the chain lock as fast as he could.

Stevie's hand closed over the seat and String jumped like a rabbit.

"Come on."

"It's late," said String, his cheeks bright pink. "I've got to go home or my Mum'll go berserk."

Stevie went on standing there with his hand on the seat. He was as quick as a monkey and at any moment the girls expected him to swing up on the railings and drop onto the bike. His hand closed tighter and tighter over the saddle as if he wouldn't mind crushing it.

"I've got to go home," said String.

Stevie shrugged. Suddenly he let go of the bike. It scraped down the railings. String stopped it. He slid it back across the yard out of Stevie's way.

Stevie turned to face him. String got on the bike and twirled the pedal.

"Thought you were going home," said Stevie.

"I am."

"What's stopping you?"

String set off. The bike wobbled. He was afraid that Stevie was going to jump out at him and push him over. The girls too expected something dreadful to happen. But Stevie did nothing. He just stood there and let String ride away. Then he swung round abruptly, brushed past the girls and headed for home.

They watched him turn the corner.

"String had a fright," said Sharon.

"Serves him right," said Vicky. "He's always on and on about that bike. He should have let Stevie have a go."

Lyn frowned. "I wouldn't like Stevie to have anything of mine. He'd never look after it. He never used to look after things when he was at our school."

"He's not so bad." Vicky nudged her and winked.

Lyn relaxed and grinned too. Stevie Baker had actually done her a favour for once. He'd got String out of the way.

"There's your Mum's car," Jenny called as the red Mini came gliding round the corner.

As soon as the car stopped, Vicky bounded forward as though String were still breathing down their necks. She pulled the door open and bundled the others inside so quickly that they all

ended up in a heap on the back seat. Lyn climbed in the front and slammed the door.

"Seat-belt on." Mum looked back over her shoulder.

"Where's the Alsatian, Mrs Harris?" asked Sharon.

Lyn stopped breathing for a moment. She glanced at Mum, but Mum was watching the traffic.

"He's at home," she puffed, easing her foot off the accelerator. "I hope he's all right. I haven't seen him since this morning."

And that was that. Lyn's small cousins, including Peter and Paul the two year-old twins, were waiting at the Wimpy, and they were far more fun to play with than even an Alsatian.

4

The Carrot-eater

IT WASN'T TILL Mum and Lyn had
dropped the others off and were almost
at their own front gate, that they had
time to talk about the guinea-pig. Mum
was smiling and pleased that the party
had gone well. She patted Lyn's knee.

"Dad'll be out in the garden playing
with that guinea-pig," she said. "You'll
see."

Mum parked the car and Lyn headed
for the house.

"Dad!" she called.

There was no answer. She went to open the back door and saw a cream and brown shape scuttle over the grass.

"Alsatian's out!" She started running towards him.

"Sh!" An arm shot out of the shed and stopped her just in time. It was Dad's. "He's enjoying himself," Dad whispered. "He'll go back to his hutch when he feels like it. My guinea-pig used to run wild."

"He'll get eaten!" Lyn looked horrified.

"No, he won't," said Dad. "Nothing ever gets over the wall into this yard. Anyway I'm only leaving him out for a few minutes."

After the first excitement Alsatian had calmly gone to nibble the tall blades of grass that grew at the foot of the wall. Dad drew Lyn over towards him. They both crouched down and Dad made small kissing noises. Alsatian looked round. A blade of grass disappeared into his mouth. He pulled at another. Dad made the noises again. Alsatian held up one paw and sniffed the air in Dad's direction. Just as Dad was going to call him for the third time, he made up his mind and came bounding over. Dad swept him up and rewarded him with a handful of dried guinea-pig food from his pocket.

"You're a clever guinea-pig," he said, "a very clever guinea-pig. You train him like that, Lyn, and he'll come to you."

Lyn took him from her father. Alsatian was pleased to see her and nosed under her chin. Lyn stroked him over and over again. She was going to make him as bold and as brave as a guinea-pig could be.

She put her hand in Dad's pocket, brought out the rest of the guinea-pig food and laid a trail across the grass. Alsatian tried to wriggle over her shoulder to see what was happening.

"Wait!" she said. When the trail was ready, she set Alsatian down at one end. "Now! Off you go!"

Alsatian sniffed and nibbled up a piece of hard grey cake. He liked that. He went on to the sunflower seed and ate that too. He sniffed at a piece of corn.

"Go on!" said Lyn.

But Alsatian got bored with the corn and the seeds. He left the trail and waddled off to find grass.

"Oh!" Lyn wrinkled her nose.

Dad laughed, rested his hand on

Lyn's shoulder and pushed himself up.

"You can't teach him too much at once. He's only been with you a day and he's learnt a lot already."

"Yes," said Lyn, "considering he's a guinea-pig."

Dad went into the house and she lay on her back to watch Alsatian eat. He was working his way along the foot of the wall. He came across to her, rested his front paws on her arm and sniffed, as if he'd forgotten who or what she was.

"Hi, Alsatian," whispered Lyn. "It's me."

Alsatian climbed on to her chest, walked right over her and slid down the other side.

Mum threw Lyn a piece of carrot. Lyn rolled over on to her elbow and held it out. Alsatian's eyes fixed on it. Lyn made kissing noises. Alsatian started moving over the grass. As he came nearer Lyn drew back her hand. She held the carrot up high.

"Come on," she said. "Sit up. Beg for it." Alsatian held one paw in the air, lifted his nose. "Beg!" Alsatian tried to climb up her arm. "Go on!"

To encourage Alsatian Lyn kept as still and as quiet as she could. That was how she heard a whisper of wheels in the back lane. It stopped just outside the yard door.

"Sh!" She sat bolt upright. Alsatian tumbled on to the grass. The carrot disappeared from his sight and he gave a squeak of dismay.

Lyn heard a slight sound of metal against stone. She snatched up Alsatian, popped him back in his hutch and ran for the door. It wasn't bolted! She sat against it.

The latch moved softly once . . . twice. Footsteps padded away. Lyn opened the door, shot through and came face to face with String. String was staring up at the top of the wall. It was an eight-foot wall and much too high for him. He looked round at Lyn as if he'd seen a ghost.

"What are you doing?" She closed the door and stood in front of it with folded arms.

String found his tongue.

"Out on my bike, aren't I?"

"You're not on your bike," said Lyn. String's bike was resting against the wall.

String shrugged. His hands were in his pockets and his shoulders hunched as if he'd just had a row at school. Lyn

knew what was wrong with him. It was Stevie Baker. String didn't like being made to look small.

She relented and nodded at the bike.

"It's a good bike," she said kindly. "It looks like new. You wouldn't think it was second-hand."

"It's not really second-hand at all," burst out String. "It belonged to my Dad's friend and he never had time to use it. It is new. Anyway it's better than pretending to have an Alsatian when you haven't really got one."

"I have!" Lyn was stung.

"Why isn't it barking?" String demanded.

"It's in the house." It wasn't really a lie. Alsatian had his own little house.

"Let's see it then."

"No!"

"You haven't got one."

"I have!" Lyn's face was like a beacon. "It's not used to strangers. It could bite you."

"I'm not scared."

"Yes, you are." Lyn drew herself up. "You are. You're scared of Stevie Baker."

"I'm not!" Two bright red spots flared up on String's cheeks. He was so angry he could hardly speak. "I . . . I'm not. I don't want him to damage my bike, that's all. That's different. That's not being scared." He snatched his bike from the wall and then, as though he were ashamed of treating it so roughly, he patted the seat.

"You should share," snapped Lyn. "You're mean, you are, String James."

"And you!" He swung on the bike and twanged the bell. Lyn backed away and Alsatian's carrot dropped from her hand. String stared at it as he rode off.

When he'd gone out of sight, Lyn gathered up the carrot and retreated into the yard. She felt hot and grumpy and a little bit silly. Alsatian was pushing his nose through the mesh of his run. Lyn gave him the carrot and he fell on it as delightedly as if he were having a party at the Wimpy. Lyn watched him gnaw away at it with his rat teeth.

"Oh, Alsatian," she said. "I wish you didn't eat carrots. I wish you ate bones and meat and that sort of thing."

5

Poor Alsatian!

LYN DANGLED A piece of bacon rind over Alsatian's hutch in the morning.

"Oh, Lyn!" laughed Mum. "He's a little guinea-pig. He doesn't eat meat."

She fetched him another piece of carrot and Alsatian was so busy eating it, he didn't even bother to lift his head when Lyn set off for school.

"Coming shopping with me tonight?" Mum called.

"No thanks," said Lyn.

"Alsatian's more interesting than the

shops, is he?" Mum rumpled her hair.

Lyn smiled. She didn't want Mum picking her up from school in case String tried to ask her questions, as he'd done the day before.

She needn't have worried, though. When the end of school came, String was off like a flash.

"Don't suppose he wants to see Stevie Baker again," said Vicky.

They were walking past the park. Lyn spotted a fresh clump of dandelion leaves growing right by the gate.

"Wait!" She crouched down and started tugging.

"What d'you want those for?" Vicky frowned.

"For Alsatian," puffed Lyn.

Vicky looked round. "There's loads growing here."

"He's only small," said Lyn. "I don't

suppose he'll eat a lot."

The dandelion leaves came away in her hand leaving a round hole in the tarmac. She put them in her satchel in case String happened to pass.

Vicky came home with her to see how Alsatian liked his new food. Alsatian was beside himself with joy. Lyn couldn't push the leaves through the wire fast enough. He tugged them out of her hand and gobbled them up in no time at all.

"I thought you said he was small and wouldn't eat much," laughed Vicky.

"We'll get you more. Don't you worry, little Alsatian," said Lyn. She moved his run on to fresh grass. Already there were three brown rectangles on the lawn where he'd eaten the grass down to the roots.

Lyn went to fetch some biscuits for

herself and Vicky from the biscuit tin, then she found a paper bag each. She made sure the yard door was bolted before setting off for the park.

"I don't want String sneaking in," she told Vicky as she slipped the front door key under the flowerpot.

"I hope he's not in the park," said Vicky. "He'll want to know why we're picking dandelion leaves, nosy thing!"

String wasn't in the park. He was out on the road on his bike. He whizzed past.

"Where are you going?" he called.

"Mind your own business," said Vicky.

String laughed and sailed round the corner.

The park was empty apart from a group of secondary schoolboys kicking a ball at the far end.

"Good!" said Lyn and she started to gather the juicy leaves at the foot of the wall as fast as she could. She packed the leaves in tight, closed the bag and twirled the ends as the greengrocer did. Vicky filled her bag too.

"Alsatian's eyes will pop out of his head when he sees this," she said.

String was still hanging around. He passed them again, riding fast and grinning at nothing in particular like a Cheshire cat.

"Snob!" yelled Vicky after him.

They turned the corner. There was no sign of the red Mini. Mum wasn't home. Lyn took the key out from under the flowerpot and let herself into the house. She glanced out of the kitchen window. Alsatian was nowhere to be seen.

"He's sleeping," laughed Vicky. "He's eaten too much."

Lyn unbolted the door and made kissing noises. She put out her arm to stop Vicky rushing forward.

"He'll come now," she said and made the noises again.

Nothing happened.

"I hope those dandelions haven't made him ill," said Vicky.

Lyn's heart gave a jump. She ran over to the hutch and opened the lid expecting to see a poor sick Alsatian. The hutch was empty!

"Alsatian's gone!"

Without a word Vicky rushed off to check the flowerpots and the old washing-up bowl in the back yard. The door of Dad's shed was shut, but Lyn opened it just in case. There was no sign of Alsatian.

With trembling hands Lyn unbolted the yard door and looked out into the lane.

"What are you looking for?" whispered Vicky.

"Perhaps an animal's taken him."

Vicky frowned. "An animal wouldn't be able to open a hutch and close it again," she said.

Lyn spun round. They stared at each other and with one voice shouted: "String!"

"The beast!" cried Lyn as she and Vicky tore down the lane towards the park.

String was just cycling out through the park gate. When he saw them, he turned round sharply.

"String!" they roared.

He didn't stop. When they got to the park, he was lounging slightly out of breath against the climbing frame.

"Where's my Alsatian?" Lyn rushed up and grabbed his arm.

"Alsatian?" grinned String. "I haven't seen an Alsatian."

"You know," said Vicky.

"No, I don't."

"String!" begged Lyn. "Guinea-pigs can die if they're frightened. If anything happens to that guinea-pig, it's your fault."

"Guinea-pig?" said String. "I thought you'd lost an Alsatian."

"His name's Alsatian," Lyn said.

"Was that all you had on your birthday?" jeered String. "One measly little guinea-pig?"

"Bring him back."

"String!" said Vicky, pointing a finger. "You give him back at once. We could go to the police about you. You shouldn't take people's keys and . . ."

"I didn't take a key," scoffed String. "I climbed over the wall."

"You didn't!" Lyn was shocked.

String laughed at her. "It's easy. The bricks are rotten."

"String!" warned Vicky. "You shouldn't steal things."

"I'm just taking your Alsatian for a walk in the park," protested String. "What's wrong with that? Anyway you shouldn't lie."

"We didn't." Vicky folded her arms. "Lyn did have an Alsatian, a guinea-pig called Alsatian."

"Where is he?" Lyn cried.

String sighed. Lazily he stretched out an arm which had a chain lock wrapped round it like a bangle.

"He's sleeping comfortably in my saddle-bag behind that rhododendron bush."

The words came out like an express train. When they'd sunk in, Lyn ran.

She rounded the rhododendron bush and stopped.

"String!" she yelled red in the face and rushing back towards him. "You're a liar, a horrible liar. Where is Alsatian?"

String pushed past her. He stopped short too. Lyn knew by his face that something terrible had happened.

"What's wrong?" Her voice was hollow.

"It's gone," String whispered, his eyes like saucers. "My bike's gone!"

No one moved. They all stood rooted

like the giant oak trees in the park. Lyn's legs felt heavy, but her head was as light as a flower blowing in the wind.

A whistle echoed across the park.

Vicky looked over her shoulder. "Stevie Baker!" She turned right round and gripped String's elbow hard. "It's Stevie Baker! And he's got your bike!"

Lyn saw Stevie Baker come riding along the path with his friend Brian trotting by his side. He was trilling the bell as he went and his legs were so short that sometimes his feet lost the pedals completely.

"Call this a bike!" he bellowed to String. "Wheelbarrow, more like."

String's mouth opened and closed, but no sound came out.

Stevie Baker swooped down the far side of the park leaving Brian way behind. The bike was going so fast, he'd lost control of the pedals and his legs were stuck out on each side like a clown's.

"He's going to ruin my bike!" String started to run.

"That's nothing," sobbed Lyn, running after him. "He's going to kill Alsatian!"

6

Alsatian Strikes Back

SOMEHOW STEVIE MANAGED to keep the bike upright till he'd reached the flat path by the side of the football pitch. They saw him bump, jerk and then slow down. Lyn kept her eyes on the saddle-bag which moved up and down like a yo-yo as she ran.

Stevie got off the bike and turned to face them with Brian beside him.

"Give my bike back," yelled String charging towards them.

"Is it really your bike?" Stevie pretended to be shocked. "Isn't it pretty? I thought it was a doll's bike. You try it, Bri."

"Give it back!" String skidded to a halt, his voice croaky.

"Just having a quick ride." Stevie watched him slyly. "What's the matter with that?" He gripped the handlebar between thumb and forefinger and rocked the bike back and forth. Lyn could just see it being dashed to the ground with poor Alsatian inside. She looked round at String, begging him with her eyes not to do anything hasty, but String had seen the danger too. He was tensed up, standing his ground.

Stevie nodded at Brian and Brian got on the bike. He rode straight at them, swerved at the last moment and headed across the grass. Stevie pushed his hands in his pockets and strolled after him. Brian was riding upright and the bike was kicking like a wild horse.

"I'm going to phone 999." Vicky stood stiffly to attention with a look of great determination on her face. "I am."

"No!" Lyn clutched at her arm.

"Why not?" Vicky raised her chin.

"If they see the police coming, they'll fling the bike down with Alsatian inside."

"They'll do that anyway," String said bitterly.

The three of them stood helpless. Brian and Stevie were up in the play area. Stevie had got on the roundabout and Brian was circling round him.

"They're not going to get away with

it," said Vicky. "I'm going to phone the police anyway." She started marching towards the gate.

Stevie saw her. He pointed. Brian sped along the path and screeched right up to Vicky. Vicky said nothing. She side-stepped on to the grass. Brian glanced quickly from her to Lyn and String.

"What's the matter?" he demanded. "Where are you going?"

Vicky turned round. She carried on walking backwards.

"I'm going to the police."

"She's going to the police!" Brian yelled over his shoulder.

"What for?" Stevie came tearing towards the bike.

Vicky raised her shoulders and refused to answer.

"It's nothing to do with you," Stevie said. "It's not your bike."

"It's not yours either," retorted Vicky.

"I wouldn't want it." Stevie's hand clamped over the seat as Brian got off. "It's pathetic. It's not a man's bike. It's too clean and shiny and neat."

He began to rock the bike. Vicky hesitated. String started forward. Stevie watched him from the corner of his eye. He rocked the bike at arm's length.

"If you break it . . ." snapped String.

"Me?" Stevie said innocently.

There was a movement inside the saddle-bag as Alsatian tried hard to keep his balance.

"It's my bike," String growled.

"Keep it!"

Stevie's knuckles went white. Lyn saw him bring his arms back ready to fling the bike away.

"Stop!" she cried and hurled herself towards him.

Stevie jumped. At the same time there came a wild desperate squeak from the saddle-bag. It gave Stevie such a shock that the bike would have fallen from his grasp of its own accord if String hadn't grabbed hold of the handlebars.

Alsatian squeaked again. He badly wanted to escape. He scratched and he clawed. He searched for a glimpse of daylight. He pushed into the corner of the bag, found an opening and pushed a brown nose out. It touched Stevie's hand.

"A rat!" Stevie screeched and shot back against Brian. Both boys tumbled on to the grass.

Alsatian slipped back into the bottom of the bag with a miserable squeak. The bag swayed and bulged as he went mad trying to batter his way out. Lyn didn't dare move. Alsatian was safer where he was for the moment.

"A rat!" wailed Stevie who was bent double clutching his hand as if a lion had taken a bite out of it.

"Did it bite you?" Brian shook him.

Stevie held out his hand. It hadn't a mark on it.

"It touched me," he whispered watching Brian with frightened eyes.

"You can get Weil's disease from rats," said Brian.

Stevie scrambled up and stared in horror at the saddle-bag. Alsatian had quietened, but his shape could be seen lurking in the corner. Stevie turned tail and ran like a rabbit towards the park gate with Brian close behind him.

As soon as they'd gone, Vicky leapt in the air like a delighted ballet-dancer.

"Don't think you'll be bothered by them again somehow," she told String.

"No." A big grin spread over String's face. He gave a huge sigh of relief and winked at Lyn. "Thanks to that ferocious Alsatian."

Lyn beamed as she rushed to open the saddle-bag.

"Alsatian!" She whispered to the bundle of fur inside.

Alsatian looked, then he stared, then suddenly he was all of a tizz clambering up the inside of the bag.

"Come on!" Lyn lifted him out and hugged him. String and Vicky gathered round.

"My hero!" said String, tapping Alsatian on the head. "You scared them." Then he took a deep breath before crouching by his bike and running his hand all over it. He bent close to study the back wheel bar, spat on his finger and rubbed.

"Is it O.K.?" Lyn asked.

"Just a bit of dirt." String's face was shining. "It's O.K." He got on his bike and away he went sailing round the edge of the park and out through the gate.

"Well, he could have waited!" Vicky plucked a dandelion leaf and offered it to Alsatian. Alsatian wouldn't take it so she draped it over Lyn's arm. Just as the three of them reached the park gate Lyn felt something tickle her arm. She looked down and saw the leaf disappearing.

She saw String too sitting on the front wall outside her house telling the whole story to an amazed Mum and Dad.

"Here he is!" he shouted, pointing to Alsatian as Lyn came up. "Here's the fiercest police dog in the world!"

Dad winked.

"Guinea-pig!" protested Lyn winking back and tucking herself and Alsatian under Dad's arm. "He's a guinea-pig, that's what he is. Honest, String! Can't you tell the difference?"